# Dear Parents:

Congratulations! Your child is taking the first steps on an exciting journey. The destination? Independent reading!

**STEP INTO READING®** will help your child get there. The program offers five steps to reading success. Each step includes fun stories and colorful art or photographs. In addition to original fiction and books with favorite characters, there are Step into Reading Non-Fiction Readers, Phonics Readers and Boxed Sets, Sticker Readers, and Comic Readers—a complete literacy program with something to interest every child.

## Learning to Read, Step by Step!

**Ready to Read   Preschool–Kindergarten**
• big type and easy words • rhyme and rhythm • picture clues
For children who know the alphabet and are eager to begin reading.

**Reading with Help   Preschool–Grade 1**
• basic vocabulary • short sentences • simple stories
For children who recognize familiar words and sound out new words with help.

**Reading on Your Own   Grades 1–3**
• engaging characters • easy-to-follow plots • popular topics
For children who are ready to read on their own.

**Reading Paragraphs   Grades 2–3**
• challenging vocabulary • short paragraphs • exciting stories
For newly independent readers who read simple sentences with confidence.

**Ready for Chapters   Grades 2–4**
• chapters • longer paragraphs • full-color art
For children who want to take the plunge into chapter books but still like colorful pictures.

**STEP INTO READING®** is designed to give every child a successful reading experience. The grade levels are only guides; children will progress through the steps at their own speed, developing confidence in their reading. The F&P Text Level on the back cover serves as another tool to help you choose the right book for your child.

Remember, a lifetime love of reading starts with a single step!

Visit us on the Web!
StepIntoReading.com
randomhousekids.com

Educators and librarians, for a variety of teaching tools, visit us at RHTeachersLibrarians.com

*Library of Congress Cataloging-in-Publication Data*
Eastman, P. D. (Philip D.), author, illustrator.
Aaron Is cool / by P. D. Eastman.
pages cm. — (Step into reading. Step 1)
"This work is adapted from Everything Happens to Aaron in the Winter by P. D. Eastman, copyright © 1967 by Penguin Random House LLC."
Summary: Aaron the alligator gets stuck in a snowball, falls through ice, and sleeps through the New Year celebration.
ISBN 978-0-553-51237-3 (trade pbk.) — ISBN 978-0-553-51238-0 (lib. bdg.) — ISBN 978-0-553-51239-7 (ebook)
[1. Ability—Fiction. 2. Winter—Fiction. 3. Alligators—Fiction. 4. Humorous stories.] I. Title.
PZ7.E1314Aax 2015 [E]—dc23 2014025950

Printed in the United States of America

10 9 8 7 6 5 4 3 2 1

This book has been officially leveled by using the F&P Text Level Gradient™ Leveling System.

WITHDRAWN

# Aaron
## Is Cool

# by P. D. Eastman

Random House New York

This is Aaron.

Aaron is an alligator.

Aaron watches his friends

make a big snowball.

# The snowball gets away!

Aaron will stop it!

Hooray!
Aaron stops
the snowball!

He looks like
a snowman!

Aaron writes his name
on the ice.

He makes a big "A."

He makes a small "a."

Oops!

What kind of letter

is that?

Aaron opens his
holiday gifts.

To Aaron from Sister Sue

To Aaron from Uncle Joe

To Aaron from Aunt Mary

# What did he get?

He got new pants
from Cousin Lucy.

He got a new shirt
from Aunt Mary.

He got a new hat
from Uncle Joe.

Nothing fits!

At last!

Overalls from Sister Sue

fit just right!

Brrr!

It is cold outside.

Aaron knows
how to stay warm.

Lots of blankets!

This curtain will make

a good blanket.

This rug is just
the right size.

Aaron is warm and comfy
on a cold winter night.

# Aaron is still warm,
# but not very comfy!

It is New Year's Eve.

Aaron is asleep.

The New Year came
and Aaron missed
the party!

# Happy New Year, Aaron!